D H Lawrence - Amores

For many of us DH Lawrence was a schoolboy hero. Who can forget sniggering in class at the mention of 'Women In Love' or 'Lady Chatterley's Lover'? Lawrence was a talented if nomadic writer whose novels were passionately received, suppressed at times and generally at odds with Establishment values. This of course did not deter him.

At his death in 1930 at the young age of 44 he was more often thought of as a pornographer but in the ensuing years he has come to be more rightly regarded as one of the most imaginative writers these shores have produced.

As well as his novels he was also a masterful poet (he wrote over 800 of them), a travel writer as well as an author of many classic short stories.

Here we publish his poetry collection 'Amores'. Once again Lawrence shows his hand as a brilliant writer. Delving into situations and peeling them back to reveal the inner heart.

Index Of Contents

TEASE

I will give you all my keys,
You shall be my châtelaine,
You shall enter as you please,
As you please shall go again.

When I hear you jingling through
All the chambers of my soul,
How I sit and laugh at you
In your vain housekeeping rôle.

Jealous of the smallest cover,
Angry at the simplest door;
Well, you anxious, inquisitive lover,

Are you pleased with what's in store?

You have fingered all my treasures,
Have you not, most curiously,
Handled all my tools and measures
And masculine machinery?

Over every single beauty
You have had your little rapture;
You have slain, as was your duty,
Every sin-mouse you could capture.

Still you are not satisfied,
Still you tremble faint reproach;
Challenge me I keep aside
Secrets that you may not broach.

Maybe yes, and maybe no,
Maybe there are secret places,
Altars barbarous below,
Elsewhere halls of high disgraces.

Maybe yes, and maybe no,
You may have it as you please,
Since I choose to keep you so,
Suppliant on your curious knees.

THE WILD COMMON

The quick sparks on the gorse bushes are leaping,
Little jets of sunlight-texture imitating flame;
Above them, exultant, the pee-wits are sweeping:
They are lords of the desolate wastes of sadness
their screamings proclaim.

Rabbits, handfuls of brown earth, lie
Low-rounded on the mournful grass they have bitten
down to the quick.
Are they asleep? Are they alive? Now see,
when I
Move my arms the hill bursts and heaves under their
spurting kick.

The common flaunts bravely; but below, from the
rushes
Crowds of glittering king-cups surge to challenge the
blossoming bushes;
There the lazy streamlet pushes
Its curious course mildly; here it wakes again, leaps,

laughs, and gushes.

Into a deep pond, an old sheep-dip,
Dark, overgrown with willows, cool, with the brook
ebbing through so slow,
Naked on the steep, soft lip
Of the bank I stand watching my own white shadow
quivering to and fro.

What if the gorse flowers shrivelled and kissing were
lost?
Without the pulsing waters, where were the marigolds
and the songs of the brook?
If my veins and my breasts with love embossed
Withered, my insolent soul would be gone like flowers
that the hot wind took.

So my soul like a passionate woman turns,
Filled with remorseful terror to the man she scorned,
and her love
For myself in my own eyes' laughter burns,
Runs ecstatic over the pliant folds rippling down to
my belly from the breast-lights above.

Over my sunlit skin the warm, clinging air,
Rich with the songs of seven larks singing at once,
goes kissing me glad.
And the soul of the wind and my blood compare
Their wandering happiness, and the wind, wasted in
liberty, drifts on and is sad.

Oh but the water loves me and folds me,
Plays with me, sways me, lifts me and sinks me as
though it were living blood,
Blood of a heaving woman who holds me,
Owning my supple body a rare glad thing, supremely
good.

STUDY

Somewhere the long mellow note of the blackbird
Quickens the unclasping hands of hazel,
Somewhere the wind-flowers fling their heads back,
Stirred by an impetuous wind. Some ways'll
All be sweet with white and blue violet.
(Hush now, hush. Where am I? Biuret)

On the green wood's edge a shy girl hovers
From out of the hazel-screen on to the grass,

Where wheeling and screaming the petulant plovers
Wave frighted. Who comes? A labourer, alas!
Oh the sunset swims in her eyes' swift pool.
(Work, work, you fool!)

Somewhere the lamp hanging low from the ceiling
Lights the soft hair of a girl as she reads,
And the red firelight steadily wheeling
Weaves the hard hands of my friend in sleep.
And the white dog snuffs the warmth, appealing
For the man to heed lest the girl shall weep.

(Tears and dreams for them; for me
Bitter science, the exams are near.
I wish I bore it more patiently.
I wish you did not wait, my dear,
For me to come: since work I must:
Though it's all the same when we are dead.
I wish I was only a bust,
All head.)

DISCORD IN CHILDHOOD

Outside the house an ash-tree hung its terrible
whips,
And at night when the wind arose, the lash of the tree
Shrieked and slashed the wind, as a ship's
Weird rigging in a storm shrieks hideously.

Within the house two voices arose in anger, a slender
lash
Whistling delirious rage, and the dreadful sound
Of a thick lash booming and bruising, until it
drowned
The other voice in a silence of blood, 'neath the noise
of the ash.

VIRGIN YOUTH

Now and again
All my body springs alive,
And the life that is polarised in my eyes,
That quivers between my eyes and mouth,
Flies like a wild thing across my body,
Leaving my eyes half-empty, and clamorous,
Filling my still breasts with a flush and a flame,
Gathering the soft ripples below my breasts

Into urgent, passionate waves,
And my soft, slumbering belly
Quivering awake with one impulse of desire,
Gathers itself fiercely together;
And my docile, fluent arms
Knotting themselves with wild strength
To clasp what they have never clasped.
Then I tremble, and go trembling
Under the wild, strange tyranny of my body,
Till it has spent itself,
And the relentless nodality of my eyes reasserts itself,
Till the bursten flood of life ebbs back to my eyes,
Back from my beautiful, lonely body
Tired and unsatisfied.

MONOLOGUE OF A MOTHER

This is the last of all, this is the last!
I must hold my hands, and turn my face to the fire,
I must watch my dead days fusing together in dross,
Shape after shape, and scene after scene from my past
Fusing to one dead mass in the sinking fire
Where the ash on the dying coals grows swiftly, like
heavy moss.

Strange he is, my son, whom I have awaited like a
lover,
Strange to me like a captive in a foreign country,
haunting
The confines and gazing out on the land where the
wind is free;
White and gaunt, with wistful eyes that hover
Always on the distance, as if his soul were chaunting
The monotonous weird of departure away from me.

Like a strange white bird blown out of the frozen
seas,
Like a bird from the far north blown with a broken
wing
Into our sooty garden, he drags and beats
From place to place perpetually, seeking release
From me, from the hand of my love which creeps up,
needing
His happiness, whilst he in displeasure retreats.

I must look away from him, for my faded eyes
Like a cringing dog at his heels offend him now,
Like a toothless hound pursuing him with my will,
Till he chafes at my crouching persistence, and a

sharp spark flies
In my soul from under the sudden frown of his brow,
As he blenches and turns away, and my heart stands
still.

This is the last, it will not be any more.
All my life I have borne the burden of myself,
All the long years of sitting in my husband's house,
Never have I said to myself as he closed the door:
"Now I am caught! You are hopelessly lost, O
Self,
You are frightened with joy, my heart, like a
frightened mouse."

Three times have I offered myself, three times rejected.
It will not be any more. No more, my son, my son!
Never to know the glad freedom of obedience, since
long ago
The angel of childhood kissed me and went. I expected
Another would take me, and now, my son, O my son,
I must sit awhile and wait, and never know
The loss of myself, till death comes, who cannot fail.

Death, in whose service is nothing of gladness, takes
me;
For the lips and the eyes of God are behind a veil.
And the thought of the lipless voice of the Father
shakes me
With fear, and fills my eyes with the tears of desire,
And my heart rebels with anguish as night draws
nigher,

IN A BOAT

See the stars, love,
In the water much clearer and brighter
Than those above us, and whiter,
Like nenuphars.

Star-shadows shine, love,
How many stars in your bowl?
How many shadows in your soul,
Only mine, love, mine?

When I move the oars, love,
See how the stars are tossed,
Distorted, the brightest lost.
So that bright one of yours, love.

The poor waters spill
The stars, waters broken, forsaken.
The heavens are not shaken, you say, love,
Its stars stand still.

There, did you see
That spark fly up at us; even
Stars are not safe in heaven.
What of yours, then, love, yours?

What then, love, if soon
Your light be tossed over a wave?
Will you count the darkness a grave,
And swoon, love, swoon?

WEEK-NIGHT SERVICE

The five old bells
Are hurrying and eagerly calling,
Imploring, protesting
They know, but clamorously falling
Into gabbling incoherence, never resting,
Like spattering showers from a bursten sky-rocket
dropping
In splashes of sound, endlessly, never stopping.

The silver moon
That somebody has spun so high
To settle the question, yes or no, has caught
In the net of the night's balloon,
And sits with a smooth bland smile up there in
the sky
Smiling at naught,
Unless the winking star that keeps her company
Makes little jests at the bells' insanity,
As if he knew aught!

The patient Night
Sits indifferent, hugged in her rags,
She neither knows nor cares
Why the old church sobs and brags;
The light distresses her eyes, and tears
Her old blue cloak, as she crouches and covers her
face,
Smiling, perhaps, if we knew it, at the bells' loud
clattering disgrace.

The wise old trees
Drop their leaves with a faint, sharp hiss of contempt,

While a car at the end of the street goes by with a
laugh;
As by degrees
The poor bells cease, and the Night is exempt,
And the stars can chaff
The ironic moon at their ease, while the dim old
church
Is peopled with shadows and sounds and ghosts that
lurch
In its cenotaph.

IRONY

Always, sweetheart,
Carry into your room the blossoming boughs of
cherry,
Almond and apple and pear diffuse with light, that
very
Soon strews itself on the floor; and keep the radiance
of spring
Fresh quivering; keep the sunny-swift March-days
waiting
In a little throng at your door, and admit the one
who is plaiting
Her hair for womanhood, and play awhile with her,
then bid her depart.

A come and go of March-day loves
Through the flower-vine, trailing screen;
A fluttering in of doves.
Then a launch abroad of shrinking doves
Over the waste where no hope is seen
Of open hands:
Dance in and out
Small-bosomed girls of the spring of love,
With a bubble of laughter, and shrilly shout
Of mirth; then the dripping of tears on your
glove.

DREAMS OLD AND NASCENT

OLD

I have opened the window to warm my hands on the
sill
Where the sunlight soaks in the stone: the afternoon
Is full of dreams, my love, the boys are all still

In a wistful dream of Lorna Doone.

The clink of the shunting engines is sharp and fine,
Like savage music striking far off, and there
On the great, uplifted blue palace, lights stir and
shine
Where the glass is domed in the blue, soft air.

There lies the world, my darling, full of wonder and
wistfulness and strange
Recognition and greetings of half-acquaint things, as
I greet the cloud
Of blue palace aloft there, among misty indefinite
dreams that range
At the back of my life's horizon, where the dreamings
of past lives crowd.

Over the nearness of Norwood Hill, through the
mellow veil
Of the afternoon glows to me the old romance of
David and Dora,
With the old, sweet, soothing tears, and laughter
that shakes the sail
Of the ship of the soul over seas where dreamed
dreams lure the unoceaned explorer.

All the bygone, hushèd years
Streaming back where the mist distils
Into forgetfulness: soft-sailing waters where fears
No longer shake, where the silk sail fills
With an unfelt breeze that ebbs over the seas, where
the storm
Of living has passed, on and on
Through the coloured iridescence that swims in the
warm
Wake of the tumult now spent and gone,
Drifts my boat, wistfully lapsing after
The mists of vanishing tears and the echo of laughter.

DREAMS OLD AND NASCENT

NASCENT

My world is a painted fresco, where coloured shapes
Of old, ineffectual lives linger blurred and warm;
An endless tapestry the past has woven drapes
The halls of my life, compelling my soul to conform.

The surface of dreams is broken,

The picture of the past is shaken and scattered.
Fluent, active figures of men pass along the railway,
and I am woken
From the dreams that the distance flattered.

Along the railway, active figures of men.
They have a secret that stirs in their limbs as they
move
Out of the distance, nearer, commanding my dreamy
world.

Here in the subtle, rounded flesh
Beats the active ecstasy.
In the sudden lifting my eyes, it is clearer,
The fascination of the quick, restless Creator moving
through the mesh
Of men, vibrating in ecstasy through the rounded
flesh.

Oh my boys, bending over your books,
In you is trembling and fusing
The creation of a new-patterned dream, dream of a
generation:
And I watch to see the Creator, the power that
patterns the dream.

The old dreams are beautiful, beloved, soft-toned,
and sure,
But the dream-stuff is molten and moving mysteriously,
Alluring my eyes; for I, am I not also dream-stuff,
Am I not quickening, diffusing myself in the pattern,
shaping and shapen?

Here in my class is the answer for the great yearning:
Eyes where I can watch the swim of old dreams
reflected on the molten metal of dreams,
Watch the stir which is rhythmic and moves them
all as a heart-beat moves the blood,
Here in the swelling flesh the great activity working,
Visible there in the change of eyes and the mobile
features.

Oh the great mystery and fascination of the unseen
Shaper,
The power of the melting, fusing Force, heat,
light, all in one,
Everything great and mysterious in one, swelling and
shaping the dream in the flesh,
As it swells and shapes a bud into blossom.

Oh the terrible ecstasy of the consciousness that I

am life!
Oh the miracle of the whole, the widespread, labouring
concentration
Swelling mankind like one bud to bring forth the
fruit of a dream,
Oh the terror of lifting the innermost I out of the
sweep of the impulse of life,
And watching the great Thing labouring through the
whole round flesh of the world;
And striving to catch a glimpse of the shape of the
coming dream,
As it quickens within the labouring, white-hot metal,
Catch the scent and the colour of the coming dream,
Then to fall back exhausted into the unconscious,
molten life!

A WINTER'S TALE

Yesterday the fields were only grey with scattered
snow,
And now the longest grass-leaves hardly emerge;
Yet her deep footsteps mark the snow, and go
On towards the pines at the hills' white verge.

I cannot see her, since the mist's white scarf
Obscures the dark wood and the dull orange sky;
But she's waiting, I know, impatient and cold, half
Sobs struggling into her frosty sigh.

Why does she come so promptly, when she must
know
That she's only the nearer to the inevitable farewell;
The hill is steep, on the snow my steps are slow
Why does she come, when she knows what I have to
tell?

EPILOGUE

Patience, little Heart.
One day a heavy, June-hot woman
Will enter and shut the door to stay.

And when your stifling heart would summon
Cool, lonely night, her roused breasts will keep the
night at bay,
Sitting in your room like two tiger-lilies
Flaming on after sunset,

Destroying the cool, lonely night with the glow of
their hot twilight;
There in the morning, still, while the fierce strange
scent comes yet
Stronger, hot and red; till you thirst for the
daffodillies
With an anguished, husky thirst that you cannot
assuage,
When the daffodillies are dead, and a woman of the
dog-days holds you in gage.
Patience, little Heart.

A BABY RUNNING BAREFOOT

When the bare feet of the baby beat across the grass
The little white feet nod like white flowers in the
wind,
They poise and run like ripples lapping across the
water;
And the sight of their white play among the grass
Is like a little robin's song, winsome,
Or as two white butterflies settle in the cup of one
flower
For a moment, then away with a flutter of wings.

I long for the baby to wander hither to me
Like a wind-shadow wandering over the water,
So that she can stand on my knee
With her little bare feet in my hands,
Cool like syringa buds,
Firm and silken like pink young peony flowers.

DISCIPLINE

It is stormy, and raindrops cling like silver bees to
the pane,
The thin sycamores in the playground are swinging
with flattened leaves;
The heads of the boys move dimly through a yellow
gloom that stains
The class; over them all the dark net of my discipline
weaves.

It is no good, dear, gentleness and forbearance, I
endured too long.
I have pushed my hands in the dark soil, under the
flower of my soul

And the gentle leaves, and have felt where the roots
are strong
Fixed in the darkness, grappling for the deep soil's
little control.

And there is the dark, my darling, where the roots
are entangled and fight
Each one for its hold on the oblivious darkness, I
know that there
In the night where we first have being, before we rise
on the light,
We are not brothers, my darling, we fight and we
do not spare.

And in the original dark the roots cannot keep,
cannot know
Any communion whatever, but they bind themselves
on to the dark,
And drawing the darkness together, crush from it a
twilight, a slow
Burning that breaks at last into leaves and a flower's
bright spark.

I came to the boys with love, my dear, but they
turned on me;
I came with gentleness, with my heart 'twixt my
hands like a bowl,
Like a loving-cup, like a grail, but they spilt it
triumphantly
And tried to break the vessel, and to violate my
soul.

But what have I to do with the boys, deep down in
my soul, my love?
I throw from out of the darkness my self like a flower
into sight,
Like a flower from out of the night-time, I lift my
face, and those
Who will may warm their hands at me, comfort this
night.

But whosoever would pluck apart my flowering shall
burn their hands,
So flowers are tender folk, and roots can only hide,
Yet my flowerings of love are a fire, and the scarlet
brands
Of my love are roses to look at, but flames to chide.

But comfort me, my love, now the fires are low,
Now I am broken to earth like a winter destroyed,
and all

Myself but a knowledge of roots, of roots in the dark
that throw
A net on the undersoil, which lies passive beneath
their thrall.

But comfort me, for henceforth my love is yours
alone,
To you alone will I offer the bowl, to you will I give
My essence only, but love me, and I will atone
To you for my general loving, atone as long as I live.

SCENT OF IRISES

A faint, sickening scent of irises
Persists all morning. Here in a jar on the table
A fine proud spike of purple irises
Rising above the class-room litter, makes me unable
To see the class's lifted and bended faces
Save in a broken pattern, amid purple and gold and
sable.

I can smell the gorgeous bog-end, in its breathless
Dazzle of may-blobs, when the marigold glare overcast
you
With fire on your cheeks and your brow and your
chin as you dipped
Your face in the marigold bunch, to touch and contrast
you,
Your own dark mouth with the bridal faint lady-smocks,
Dissolved on the golden sorcery you should not
outlast.

You amid the bog-end's yellow incantation,
You sitting in the cowslips of the meadow above,
Me, your shadow on the bog-flame, flowery may-blobs,
Me full length in the cowslips, muttering you love;
You, your soul like a lady-smock, lost, evanescent,
You with your face all rich, like the sheen of a
dove.

You are always asking, do I remember, remember
The butter-cup bog-end where the flowers rose up
And kindled you over deep with a cast of gold?
You ask again, do the healing days close up
The open darkness which then drew us in,
The dark which then drank up our brimming cup.

You upon the dry, dead beech-leaves, in the fire of
night

Burnt like a sacrifice; you invisible;
Only the fire of darkness, and the scent of you!
And yes, thank God, it still is possible
The healing days shall close the darkness up
Wherein we fainted like a smoke or dew.

Like vapour, dew, or poison. Now, thank God,
The fire of night is gone, and your face is ash
Indistinguishable on the grey, chill day;
The night has burnt us out, at last the good
Dark fire burns on untroubled, without clash
Of you upon the dead leaves saying me Yea.

THE PROPHET

Ah, my darling, when over the purple horizon shall
loom
The shrouded mother of a new idea, men hide their
faces,
Cry out and fend her off, as she seeks her procreant
groom,
Wounding themselves against her, denying her
fecund embraces.

LAST WORDS TO MIRIAM

Yours is the shame and sorrow
But the disgrace is mine;
Your love was dark and thorough,
Mine was the love of the sun for a flower
He creates with his shine.

I was diligent to explore you,
Blossom you stalk by stalk,
Till my fire of creation bore you
Shrivelling down in the final dour
Anguish, then I suffered a balk.

I knew your pain, and it broke
My fine, craftsman's nerve;
Your body quailed at my stroke,
And my courage failed to give you the last
Fine torture you did deserve.

You are shapely, you are adorned,
But opaque and dull in the flesh,
Who, had I but pierced with the thorned

Fire-threshing anguish, were fused and cast
In a lovely illumined mesh.

Like a painted window: the best
Suffering burnt through your flesh,
Undrossed it and left it blest
With a quivering sweet wisdom of grace: but
now
Who shall take you afresh?

Now who will burn you free
From your body's terrors and dross,
Since the fire has failed in me?
What man will stoop in your flesh to plough
The shrieking cross?

A mute, nearly beautiful thing
Is your face, that fills me with shame
As I see it hardening,
Warping the perfect image of God,
And darkening my eternal fame.

MYSTERY

Now I am all
One bowl of kisses,
Such as the tall
Slim votaresses
Of Egypt filled
For a God's excesses.

I lift to you
My bowl of kisses,
And through the temple's
Blue recesses
Cry out to you
In wild caresses.

And to my lips'
Bright crimson rim
The passion slips,
And down my slim
White body drips
The shining hymn.

And still before
The altar I
Exult the bowl
Brimful, and cry

To you to stoop
And drink, Most High.

Oh drink me up
That I may be
Within your cup
Like a mystery,
Like wine that is still
In ecstasy.

Glimmering still
In ecstasy,
Commingled wines
Of you and me
In one fulfil
The mystery.

PATIENCE

A wind comes from the north
Blowing little flocks of birds
Like spray across the town,
And a train, roaring forth,
Rushes stampeding down
With cries and flying curds
Of steam, out of the darkening north.

Whither I turn and set
Like a needle steadfastly,
Waiting ever to get
The news that she is free;
But ever fixed, as yet,
To the lode of her agony.

BALLAD OF ANOTHER OPHELIA

Oh the green glimmer of apples in the orchard,
Lamps in a wash of rain!
Oh the wet walk of my brown hen through the stack-yard,
Oh tears on the window pane!

Nothing now will ripen the bright green apples,
Full of disappointment and of rain,
Brackish they will taste, of tears, when the yellow
dapples
Of autumn tell the withered tale again.

All round the yard it is cluck, my brown hen,
Cluck, and the rain-wet wings,
Cluck, my marigold bird, and again
Cluck for your yellow darlings.

For the grey rat found the gold thirteen
Huddled away in the dark,
Flutter for a moment, oh the beast is quick and
keen,
Extinct one yellow-fluffy spark.

Once I had a lover bright like running water,
Once his face was laughing like the sky;
Open like the sky looking down in all its laughter
On the buttercups, and the buttercups was I.

What, then, is there hidden in the skirts of all the
blossom?
What is peeping from your wings, oh mother
hen?
'Tis the sun who asks the question, in a lovely haste
for wisdom;
What a lovely haste for wisdom is in men!

Yea, but it is cruel when undressed is all the blossom,
And her shift is lying white upon the floor,
That a grey one, like a shadow, like a rat, a thief, a
rain-storm,
Creeps upon her then and gathers in his store.

Oh the grey garner that is full of half-grown apples,
Oh the golden sparkles laid extinct!
And oh, behind the cloud-sheaves, like yellow autumn
dapples,
Did you see the wicked sun that winked!

RESTLESSNESS

At the open door of the room I stand and look at
the night,
Hold my hand to catch the raindrops, that slant into
sight,
Arriving grey from the darkness above suddenly into
the light of the room.
I will escape from the hollow room, the box of light,
And be out in the bewildering darkness, which is
always fecund, which might
Mate my hungry soul with a germ of its womb.

I will go out to the night, as a man goes down to the
shore
To draw his net through the surfs thin line, at the
dawn before
The sun warms the sea, little, lonely and sad, sifting
the sobbing tide.
I will sift the surf that edges the night, with my net,
the four
Strands of my eyes and my lips and my hands and my
feet, sifting the store
Of flotsam until my soul is tired or satisfied.

I will catch in my eyes' quick net
The faces of all the women as they go past,
Bend over them with my soul, to cherish the wet
Cheeks and wet hair a moment, saying: "Is it
you?"
Looking earnestly under the dark umbrellas, held
fast
Against the wind; and if, where the lamplight
blew
Its rainy swill about us, she answered me
With a laugh and a merry wildness that it was she
Who was seeking me, and had found me at last to
free
Me now from the stunting bonds of my chastity,
How glad I should be!

Moving along in the mysterious ebb of the night
Pass the men whose eyes are shut like anemones in a
dark pool;
Why don't they open with vision and speak to me,
what have they in sight?
Why do I wander aimless among them, desirous
fool?

I can always linger over the huddled books on the
stalls,
Always gladden my amorous fingers with the touch
of their leaves,
Always kneel in courtship to the shelves in the
doorways, where falls
The shadow, always offer myself to one mistress,
who always receives.

But oh, it is not enough, it is all no good.
There is something I want to feel in my running
blood,
Something I want to touch; I must hold my face to
the rain,
I must hold my face to the wind, and let it explain

Me its life as it hurries in secret.
I will trail my hands again through the drenched,
cold leaves
Till my hands are full of the chillness and touch of
leaves,
Till at length they induce me to sleep, and to forget.

A BABY ASLEEP AFTER PAIN

As a drenched, drowned bee
Hangs numb and heavy from a bending flower,
So clings to me
My baby, her brown hair brushed with wet tears
And laid against her cheek;
Her soft white legs hanging heavily over my arm
Swinging heavily to my movement as I walk.
My sleeping baby hangs upon my life,
Like a burden she hangs on me.
She has always seemed so light,
But now she is wet with tears and numb with pain
Even her floating hair sinks heavily,
Reaching downwards;
As the wings of a drenched, drowned bee
Are a heaviness, and a weariness.

ANXIETY

The hoar-frost crumbles in the sun,
The crisping steam of a train
Melts in the air, while two black birds
Sweep past the window again.

Along the vacant road, a red
Bicycle approaches; I wait
In a thaw of anxiety, for the boy
To leap down at our gate.

He has passed us by; but is it
Relief that starts in my breast?
Or a deeper bruise of knowing that still
She has no rest.

THE PUNISHER

I have fetched the tears up out of the little wells,

Scooped them up with small, iron words,
Dripping over the runnels.

The harsh, cold wind of my words drove on, and still
I watched the tears on the guilty cheek of the boys
Glitter and spill.

Cringing Pity, and Love, white-handed, came
Hovering about the Judgment which stood in my
eyes,
Whirling a flame.

The tears are dry, and the cheeks' young fruits are
fresh
With laughter, and clear the exonerated eyes, since
pain
Beat through the flesh.

The Angel of Judgment has departed again to the
Nearness.
Desolate I am as a church whose lights are put out.
And night enters in drearness.

The fire rose up in the bush and blazed apace,
The thorn-leaves crackled and twisted and sweated in
anguish;
Then God left the place.

Like a flower that the frost has hugged and let go,
my head
Is heavy, and my heart beats slowly, laboriously,
My strength is shed.

THE END

If I could have put you in my heart,
If but I could have wrapped you in myself,
How glad I should have been!
And now the chart
Of memory unrolls again to me
The course of our journey here, before we had to
part.

And oh, that you had never, never been
Some of your selves, my love, that some
Of your several faces I had never seen!
And still they come before me, and they go,
And I cry aloud in the moments that intervene.

And oh, my love, as I rock for you to-night,
And have not any longer any hope
To heal the suffering, or make requite
For all your life of asking and despair,
I own that some of me is dead to-night.

THE BRIDE

My love looks like a girl to-night,
But she is old.
The plaits that lie along her pillow
Are not gold,
But threaded with filigree,
And uncanny cold.

She looks like a young maiden, since her brow
Is smooth and fair,
Her cheeks are very smooth, her eyes are closed,
She sleeps a rare
Still winsome sleep, so still, and so composed.

Nay, but she sleeps like a bride, and dreams her
dreams
Of perfect things.
She lies at last, the darling, in the shape of her dream,
And her dead mouth sings
By its shape, like the thrushes in clear evenings.

THE VIRGIN MOTHER

My little love, my darling,
You were a doorway to me;
You let me out of the confines
Into this strange countrie,
Where people are crowded like thistles,
Yet are shapely and comely to see.

My little love, my dearest
Twice have you issued me,
Once from your womb, sweet mother,
Once from myself, to be
Free of all hearts, my darling,
Of each heart's home-life free.

And so, my love, my mother,
I shall always be true to you;
Twice I am born, my dearest,

To life, and to death, in you;
And this is the life hereafter
Wherein I am true.

I kiss you good-bye, my darling,
Our ways are different now;
You are a seed in the night-time,
I am a man, to plough
The difficult glebe of the future
For God to endow.

I kiss you good-bye, my dearest,
It is finished between us here.
Oh, if I were calm as you are,
Sweet and still on your bier!
God, if I had not to leave you
Alone, my dear!

Let the last word be uttered,
Oh grant the farewell is said!
Spare me the strength to leave you
Now you are dead.
I must go, but my soul lies helpless
Beside your bed.

AT THE WINDOW

The pine-trees bend to listen to the autumn wind
as it mutters
Something which sets the black poplars ashake with
hysterical laughter;
While slowly the house of day is closing its eastern
shutters.

Further down the valley the clustered tombstones
recede,
Winding about their dimness the mist's grey
cerements, after
The street lamps in the darkness have suddenly
started to bleed.

The leaves fly over the window and utter a word as
they pass
To the face that leans from the darkness, intent, with
two dark-filled eyes
That watch for ever earnestly from behind the window
glass.

DRUNK

Too far away, oh love, I know,
To save me from this haunted road,
Whose lofty roses break and blow
On a night-sky bent with a load

Of lights: each solitary rose,
Each arc-lamp golden does expose
Ghost beyond ghost of a blossom, shows
Night blenched with a thousand snows.

Of hawthorn and of lilac trees,
White lilac; shows discoloured night
Dripping with all the golden lees
Laburnum gives back to light

And shows the red of hawthorn set
On high to the purple heaven of night,
Like flags in blenched blood newly wet,
Blood shed in the noiseless fight.

Of life for love and love for life,
Of hunger for a little food,
Of kissing, lost for want of a wife
Long ago, long ago wooed.

Too far away you are, my love,
To steady my brain in this phantom show
That passes the nightly road above
And returns again below.

The enormous cliff of horse-chestnut trees
Has poised on each of its ledges
An erect small girl looking down at me;
White-night-gowned little chits I see,
And they peep at me over the edges
Of the leaves as though they would leap, should
I call
Them down to my arms;
"But, child, you're too small for me, too small
Your little charms."

White little sheaves of night-gowned maids,
Some other will thresh you out!
And I see leaning from the shades
A lilac like a lady there, who braids
Her white mantilla about
Her face, and forward leans to catch the sight
Of a man's face,

Gracefully sighing through the white
Flowery mantilla of lace.

And another lilac in purple veiled
Discreetly, all recklessly calls
In a low, shocking perfume, to know who has hailed
Her forth from the night: my strength has failed
In her voice, my weak heart falls:
Oh, and see the laburnum shimmering
Her draperies down,
As if she would slip the gold, and glimmering
White, stand naked of gown.

.   .   .   .   .   .

The pageant of flowery trees above
The street pale-passionate goes,
And back again down the pavement, Love
In a lesser pageant flows.

Two and two are the folk that walk,
They pass in a half embrace
Of linkèd bodies, and they talk
With dark face leaning to face.

Come then, my love, come as you will
Along this haunted road,
Be whom you will, my darling, I shall
Keep with you the troth I trowed.

SORROW

Why does the thin grey strand
Floating up from the forgotten
Cigarette between my fingers,
Why does it trouble me?

Ah, you will understand;
When I carried my mother downstairs,
A few times only, at the beginning
Of her soft-foot malady,

I should find, for a reprimand
To my gaiety, a few long grey hairs
On the breast of my coat; and one by one
I let them float up the dark chimney.

DOLOR OF AUTUMN

The acrid scents of autumn,
Reminiscent of slinking beasts, make me fear
Everything, tear-trembling stars of autumn
And the snore of the night in my ear.

For suddenly, flush-fallen,
All my life, in a rush
Of shedding away, has left me
Naked, exposed on the bush.

I, on the bush of the globe,
Like a newly-naked berry, shrink
Disclosed: but I also am prowling
As well in the scents that slink

Abroad: I in this naked berry
Of flesh that stands dismayed on the bush;
And I in the stealthy, brindled odours
Prowling about the lush

And acrid night of autumn;
My soul, along with the rout,
Rank and treacherous, prowling,
Disseminated out.

For the night, with a great breath intaken,
Has taken my spirit outside
Me, till I reel with disseminated consciousness,
Like a man who has died.

At the same time I stand exposed
Here on the bush of the globe,
A newly-naked berry of flesh
For the stars to probe.

THE INHERITANCE

Sunce you did depart
Out of my reach, my darling,
Into the hidden,
I see each shadow start
With recognition, and I
Am wonder-ridden.

I am dazed with the farewell,
But I scarcely feel your loss.
You left me a gift

Of tongues, so the shadows tell
Me things, and silences toss
Me their drift.

You sent me a cloven fire
Out of death, and it burns in the draught
Of the breathing hosts,
Kindles the darkening pyre
For the sorrowful, till strange brands waft
Like candid ghosts.

Form after form, in the streets
Waves like a ghost along,
Kindled to me;
The star above the house-top greets
Me every eve with a long
Song fierily.

All day long, the town
Glimmers with subtle ghosts
Going up and down
In a common, prison-like dress;
But their daunted looking flickers
To me, and I answer, Yes!

So I am not lonely nor sad
Although bereaved of you,
My little love.
I move among a kinsfolk clad
With words, but the dream shows through
As they move.

SILENCE

Since I lost you I am silence-haunted,
Sounds wave their little wings
A moment, then in weariness settle
On the flood that soundless swings.

Whether the people in the street
Like pattering ripples go by,
Or whether the theatre sighs and sighs
With a loud, hoarse sigh:

Or the wind shakes a ravel of light
Over the dead-black river,
Or night's last echoing
Makes the daybreak shiver:

I feel the silence waiting
To take them all up again
In its vast completeness, enfolding
The sound of men.

LISTENING

I listen to the stillness of you,
My dear, among it all;
I feel your silence touch my words as I talk,
And take them in thrall.

My words fly off a forge
The length of a spark;
I see the night-sky easily sip them
Up in the dark.

The lark sings loud and glad,
Yet I am not loth
That silence should take the song and the bird
And lose them both.

A train goes roaring south,
The steam-flag flying;
I see the stealthy shadow of silence
Alongside going.

And off the forge of the world,
Whirling in the draught of life,
Go sparks of myriad people, filling
The night with strife.

Yet they never change the darkness
Or blench it with noise;
Alone on the perfect silence
The stars are buoys.

BROODING GRIEF

A yellow leaf from the darkness
Hops like a frog before me.
Why should I start and stand still?

I was watching the woman that bore me
Stretched in the brindled darkness
Of the sick-room, rigid with will
To die: and the quick leaf tore me

Back to this rainy swill
Of leaves and lamps and traffic mingled before me.

LOTUS HURT BY THE COLD

How many times, like lotus lilies risen
Upon the surface of a river, there
Have risen floating on my blood the rare
Soft glimmers of my hope escaped from prison.

So I am clothed all over with the light
And sensitive beautiful blossoming of passion;
Till naked for her in the finest fashion
The flowers of all my mud swim into sight.

And then I offer all myself unto
This woman who likes to love me: but she turns
A look of hate upon the flower that burns
To break and pour her out its precious dew.

And slowly all the blossom shuts in pain,
And all the lotus buds of love sink over
To die unopened: when my moon-faced lover,
Kind on the weight of suffering, smiles again.

MALADE

The sick grapes on the chair by the bed lie prone;
at the window
The tassel of the blind swings gently, tapping the
pane,
As a little wind comes in.
The room is the hollow rind of a fruit, a gourd
Scooped out and dry, where a spider,
Folded in its legs as in a bed,
Lies on the dust, watching where is nothing to see
but twilight and walls.

And if the day outside were mine! What is the day
But a grey cave, with great grey spider-cloths
hanging
Low from the roof, and the wet dust falling softly
from them
Over the wet dark rocks, the houses, and over
The spiders with white faces, that scuttle on the
floor of the cave!
I am choking with creeping, grey confinedness.

But somewhere birds, beside a lake of light, spread wings
Larger than the largest fans, and rise in a stream upwards
And upwards on the sunlight that rains invisible,
So that the birds are like one wafted feather,
Small and ecstatic suspended over a vast spread country.

LIAISON

A big bud of moon hangs out of the twilight,
Star-spiders spinning their thread
Hang high suspended, withouten respite
Watching us overhead.

Come then under the trees, where the leaf-cloths
Curtain us in so dark
That here we're safe from even the ermin-moth's
Flitting remark.

Here in this swarthy, secret tent,
Where black boughs flap the ground,
You shall draw the thorn from my discontent,
Surgeon me sound.

This rare, rich night! For in here
Under the yew-tree tent
The darkness is loveliest where I could sear
You like frankincense into scent.

Here not even the stars can spy us,
Not even the white moths write
With their little pale signs on the wall, to try us
And set us affright.

Kiss but then the dust from off my lips,
But draw the turgid pain
From my breast to your bosom, eclipse
My soul again.

Waste me not, I beg you, waste
Not the inner night:
Taste, oh taste and let me taste
The core of delight.

TROTH WITH THE DEAD

The moon is broken in twain, and half a moon
Before me lies on the still, pale floor of the sky;
The other half of the broken coin of troth
Is buried away in the dark, where the still dead lie.
They buried her half in the grave when they laid her
away;
I had pushed it gently in among the thick of her hair
Where it gathered towards the plait, on that very
last day;
And like a moon in secret it is shining there.

My half shines in the sky, for a general sign
Of the troth with the dead I pledged myself to keep;
Turning its broken edge to the dark, it shines indeed
Like the sign of a lover who turns to the dark of
sleep.
Against my heart the inviolate sleep breaks still
In darkened o'waves whose breaking echoes o'er
The wondering world of my wakeful day, till I'm
lost
In the midst of the places I knew so well before.

DISSOLUTE

Many years have I still to burn, detained
Like a candle flame on this body; but I enshrine
A darkness within me, a presence which sleeps
contained
In my flame of living, her soul enfolded in mine.

And through these years, while I burn on the fuel of
life,
What matter the stuff I lick up in my living flame,
Seeing I keep in the fire-core, inviolate,
A night where she dreams my dreams for me, ever
the same.

SUBMERGENCE

When along the pavement,
Palpitating flames of life,
People flicker round me,
I forget my bereavement,
The gap in the great constellation,
The place where a star used to be.

Nay, though the pole-star
Is blown out like a candle,
And all the heavens are wandering in disarray,
Yet when pleiads of people are
Deployed around me, and I see
The street's long outstretched Milky Way,

When people flicker down the pavement,
I forget my bereavement.

THE ENKINDLED SPRING

This spring as it comes bursts up in bonfires green,
Wild puffing of emerald trees, and flame-filled bushes,
Thorn-blossom lifting in wreaths of smoke between
Where the wood fumes up and the watery, flickering
rushes.

I am amazed at this spring, this conflagration
Of green fires lit on the soil of the earth, this blaze
Of growing, and sparks that puff in wild gyration,
Faces of people streaming across my gaze.

And I, what fountain of fire am I among
This leaping combustion of spring? My spirit is
tossed
About like a shadow buffeted in the throng
Of flames, a shadow that's gone astray, and is lost.

REPROACH

Had I but known yesterday,
Helen, you could discharge the ache
Out of the cloud;
Had I known yesterday you could take
The turgid electric ache away,
Drink it up with your proud
White body, as lovely white lightning
Is drunk from an agonised sky by the earth,
I might have hated you, Helen.

But since my limbs gushed full of fire,
Since from out of my blood and bone
Poured a heavy flame
To you, earth of my atmosphere, stone
Of my steel, lovely white flint of desire,

You have no name.
Earth of my swaying atmosphere,
Substance of my inconstant breath,
I cannot but cleave to you.

Since you have drunken up the drear
Painful electric storm, and death
Is washed from the blue
Of my eyes, I see you beautiful.
You are strong and passive and beautiful,
I come like winds that uncertain hover;
But you
Are the earth I hover over.

THE HANDS OF THE BETROTHED

Her tawny eyes are onyx of thoughtlessness,
Hardened they are like gems in ancient modesty;
Yea, and her mouth's prudent and crude caress
Means even less than her many words to me.

Though her kiss betrays me also this, this only
Consolation, that in her lips her blood at climax
clips
Two wild, dumb paws in anguish on the lonely
Fruit of my heart, ere down, rebuked, it slips.

I know from her hardened lips that still her heart is
Hungry for me, yet if I put my hand in her breast
She puts me away, like a saleswoman whose mart is
Endangered by the pilferer on his quest.

But her hands are still the woman, the large, strong
hands
Heavier than mine, yet like leverets caught in
steel
When I hold them; my still soul understands
Their dumb confession of what her sort must feel.

For never her hands come nigh me but they lift
Like heavy birds from the morning stubble, to
settle
Upon me like sleeping birds, like birds that shift
Uneasily in their sleep, disturbing my mettle.

How caressingly she lays her hand on my knee,
How strangely she tries to disown it, as it sinks
In my flesh and bone and forages into me,
How it stirs like a subtle stoat, whatever she

thinks!

And often I see her clench her fingers tight
And thrust her fists suppressed in the folds of her
skirt;
And sometimes, how she grasps her arms with her
bright
Big hands, as if surely her arms did hurt.

And I have seen her stand all unaware
Pressing her spread hands over her breasts, as she
Would crush their mounds on her heart, to kill in
there
The pain that is her simple ache for me.

Her strong hands take my part, the part of a man
To her; she crushes them into her bosom deep
Where I should lie, and with her own strong
span
Closes her arms, that should fold me in sleep.

Ah, and she puts her hands upon the wall,
Presses them there, and kisses her bright hands,
Then lets her black hair loose, the darkness fall
About her from her maiden-folded bands.

And sits in her own dark night of her bitter hair
Dreaming, God knows of what, for to me she's
the same
Betrothed young lady who loves me, and takes care
Of her womanly virtue and of my good name.

EXCURSION

I wonder, can the night go by;
Can this shot arrow of travel fly
Shaft-golden with light, sheer into the sky
Of a dawned to-morrow,
Without ever sleep delivering us
From each other, or loosing the dolorous
Unfruitful sorrow!

What is it then that you can see
That at the window endlessly
You watch the red sparks whirl and flee
And the night look through?
Your presence peering lonelily there
Oppresses me so, I can hardly bear
To share the train with you.

You hurt my heart-beats' privacy;
I wish I could put you away from me;
I suffocate in this intimacy,
For all that I love you;
How I have longed for this night in the train,
Yet now every fibre of me cries in pain
To God to remove you.

But surely my soul's best dream is still
That one night pouring down shall swill
Us away in an utter sleep, until
We are one, smooth-rounded.
Yet closely bitten in to me
Is this armour of stiff reluctancy
That keeps me impounded.

So, dear love, when another night
Pours on us, lift your fingers white
And strip me naked, touch me light,
Light, light all over.
For I ache most earnestly for your touch,
Yet I cannot move, however much
I would be your lover.

Night after night with a blemish of day
Unblown and unblossomed has withered away;
Come another night, come a new night, say
Will you pluck me apart?
Will you open the amorous, aching bud
Of my body, and loose the burning flood
That would leap to you from my heart?

PERFIDY

Hollow rang the house when I knocked on the door,
And I lingered on the threshold with my hand
Upraised to knock and knock once more:
Listening for the sound of her feet across the floor,
Hollow re-echoed my heart.

The low-hung lamps stretched down the road
With shadows drifting underneath,
With a music of soft, melodious feet
Quickening my hope as I hastened to meet
The low-hung light of her eyes.

The golden lamps down the street went out,
The last car trailed the night behind;

And I in the darkness wandered about
With a flutter of hope and of dark-shut doubt
In the dying lamp of my love.

Two brown ponies trotting slowly
Stopped at a dim-lit trough to drink:
The dark van drummed down the distance slowly;
While the city stars so dim and holy
Drew nearer to search through the streets.

A hastening car swept shameful past,
I saw her hid in the shadow,
I saw her step to the curb, and fast
Run to the silent door, where last
I had stood with my hand uplifted.
She clung to the door in her haste to enter,
Entered, and quickly cast
It shut behind her, leaving the street aghast.

A SPIRITUAL WOMAN

Close your eyes, my love, let me make you blind;
They have taught you to see
Only a mean arithmetic on the face of things,
A cunning algebra in the faces of men,
And God like geometry
Completing his circles, and working cleverly.

I'll kiss you over the eyes till I kiss you blind;
If I can, if any one could.
Then perhaps in the dark you'll have got what you
want to find.
You've discovered so many bits, with your clever
eyes,
And I'm a kaleidoscope
That you shake and shake, and yet it won't come to
your mind.
Now stop carping at me. But God, how I hate you!
Do you fear I shall swindle you?
Do you think if you take me as I am, that that will
abate you
Somehow? so sad, so intrinsic, so spiritual, yet so
cautious, you
Must have me all in your will and your consciousness
I hate you.

MATING

Round clouds roll in the arms of the wind,
The round earth rolls in a clasp of blue sky,
And see, where the budding hazels are thinned,
The wild anemones lie
In undulating shivers beneath the wind.

Over the blue of the waters ply
White ducks, a living flotilla of cloud;
And, look you, floating just thereby,
The blue-gleamed drake stems proud
Like Abraham, whose seed should multiply.

In the lustrous gleam of the water, there
Scramble seven toads across the silk, obscure leaves,
Seven toads that meet in the dusk to share
The darkness that interweaves
The sky and earth and water and live things everywhere.

Look now, through the woods where the beech-green
spurts
Like a storm of emerald snow, look, see
A great bay stallion dances, skirts
The bushes sumptuously,
Going outward now in the spring to his brief deserts.

Ah love, with your rich, warm face aglow,
What sudden expectation opens you
So wide as you watch the catkins blow
Their dust from the birch on the blue
Lift of the pulsing wind, ah, tell me you know!

Ah, surely! Ah, sure from the golden sun
A quickening, masculine gleam floats in to all
Us creatures, people and flowers undone,
Lying open under his thrall,
As he begets the year in us. What, then, would you
shun?

Why, I should think that from the earth there fly
Fine thrills to the neighbour stars, fine yellow beams
Thrown lustily off from our full-blown, high
Bursting globe of dreams,
To quicken the spheres that are virgin still in the sky.

Do you not hear each morsel thrill
With joy at travelling to plant itself within
The expectant one, therein to instil
New rapture, new shape to win,
From the thick of life wake up another will?

Surely, and if that I would spill
The vivid, ah, the fiery surplus of life,
From off my brimming measure, to fill
You, and flush you rife
With increase, do you call it evil, and always evil?

A LOVE SONG

Reject me not if I should say to you
I do forget the sounding of your voice,
I do forget your eyes that searching through
The mists perceive our marriage, and rejoice.

Yet, when the apple-blossom opens wide
Under the pallid moonlight's fingering,
I see your blanched face at my breast, and hide
My eyes from diligent work, malingering.

Ah, then, upon my bedroom I do draw
The blind to hide the garden, where the moon
Enjoys the open blossoms as they straw
Their beauty for his taking, boon for boon.

And I do lift my aching arms to you,
And I do lift my anguished, avid breast,
And I do weep for very pain of you,
And fling myself at the doors of sleep, for rest.

And I do toss through the troubled night for you,
Dreaming your yielded mouth is given to mine,
Feeling your strong breast carry me on into
The peace where sleep is stronger even than wine.

BROTHER AND SISTER

The shorn moon trembling indistinct on her path,
Frail as a scar upon the pale blue sky,
Draws towards the downward slope; some sorrow hath
Worn her down to the quick, so she faintly fares
Along her foot-searched way without knowing why
She creeps persistent down the sky's long stairs.

Some say they see, though I have never seen,
The dead moon heaped within the new moon's arms;
For surely the fragile, fine young thing had been
Too heavily burdened to mount the heavens so.

But my heart stands still, as a new, strong dread
alarms
Me; might a young girl be heaped with such shadow
of woe?

Since Death from the mother moon has pared us
down to the quick,
And cast us forth like shorn, thin moons, to travel
An uncharted way among the myriad thick
Strewn stars of silent people, and luminous litter
Of lives which sorrows like mischievous dark mice
chavel
To nought, diminishing each star's glitter,

Since Death has delivered us utterly, naked and
white,
Since the month of childhood is over, and we stand
alone,
Since the beloved, faded moon that set us alight
Is delivered from us and pays no heed though we
moan
In sorrow, since we stand in bewilderment, strange
And fearful to sally forth down the sky's long range.

We may not cry to her still to sustain us here,
We may not hold her shadow back from the dark.
Oh, let us here forget, let us take the sheer
Unknown that lies before us, bearing the ark
Of the covenant onwards where she cannot go.
Let us rise and leave her now, she will never know.

AFTER MANY DAYS

I wonder if with you, as it is with me,
If under your slipping words, that easily flow
About you as a garment, easily,
Your violent heart beats to and fro!

Long have I waited, never once confessed,
Even to myself, how bitter the separation;
Now, being come again, how make the best
Reparation?

If I could cast this clothing off from me,
If I could lift my naked self to you,
Or if only you would repulse me, a wound would be
Good; it would let the ache come through.

But that you hold me still so kindly cold

Aloof my flaming heart will not allow;
Yea, but I loathe you that you should withhold
Your pleasure now.

BLUE

The earth again like a ship steams out of the dark
sea over
The edge of the blue, and the sun stands up to see
us glide
Slowly into another day; slowly the rover
Vessel of darkness takes the rising tide.

I, on the deck, am startled by this dawn confronting
Me who am issued amazed from the darkness,
stripped
And quailing here in the sunshine, delivered from
haunting
The night unsounded whereon our days are shipped.

Feeling myself undawning, the day's light playing
upon me,
I who am substance of shadow, I all compact
Of the stuff of the night, finding myself all wrongly
Among the crowds of things in the sunshine jostled
and racked.

I with the night on my lips, I sigh with the silence
of death;
And what do I care though the very stones should
cry me unreal, though the clouds
Shine in conceit of substance upon me, who am less
than the rain.
Do I not know the darkness within them? What
are they but shrouds?

The clouds go down the sky with a wealthy ease
Casting a shadow of scorn upon me for my share in
death; but I
Hold my own in the midst of them, darkling, defy
The whole of the day to extinguish the shadow I lift
on the breeze.

Yea, though the very clouds have vantage over
me,
Enjoying their glancing flight, though my love is
dead,
I still am not homeless here, I've a tent by day
Of darkness where she sleeps on her perfect bed.

And I know the host, the minute sparkling of darkness
Which vibrates untouched and virile through the
grandeur of night,
But which, when dawn crows challenge, assaulting
the vivid motes
Of living darkness, bursts fretfully, and is bright:

Runs like a fretted arc-lamp into light,
Stirred by conflict to shining, which else
Were dark and whole with the night.

Runs to a fret of speed like a racing wheel,
Which else were aslumber along with the whole
Of the dark, swinging rhythmic instead of a-reel.

Is chafed to anger, bursts into rage like thunder;
Which else were a silent grasp that held the
heavens
Arrested, beating thick with wonder.

Leaps like a fountain of blue sparks leaping
In a jet from out of obscurity,
Which erst was darkness sleeping.

Runs into streams of bright blue drops,
Water and stones and stars, and myriads
Of twin-blue eyes, and crops

Of floury grain, and all the hosts of day,
All lovely hosts of ripples caused by fretting
The Darkness into play.

SNAP-DRAGON

She bade me follow to her garden, where
The mellow sunlight stood as in a cup
Between the old grey walls; I did not dare
To raise my face, I did not dare look up,
Lest her bright eyes like sparrows should fly in
My windows of discovery, and shrill "Sin."

So with a downcast mien and laughing voice
I followed, followed the swing of her white dress
That rocked in a lilt along: I watched the poise
Of her feet as they flew for a space, then paused to
press
The grass deep down with the royal burden of her:
And gladly I'd offered my breast to the tread of her.

"I like to see," she said, and she crouched her down,
She sunk into my sight like a settling bird;
And her bosom couched in the confines of her gown
Like heavy birds at rest there, softly stirred
By her measured breaths: "I like to see," said she,
"The snap-dragon put out his tongue at me."

She laughed, she reached her hand out to the flower,
Closing its crimson throat. My own throat in her power
Strangled, my heart swelled up so full
As if it would burst its wine-skin in my throat,
Choke me in my own crimson. I watched her pull
The gorge of the gaping flower, till the blood did float

Over my eyes, and I was blind
Her large brown hand stretched over
The windows of my mind;
And there in the dark I did discover
Things I was out to find:
My Grail, a brown bowl twined
With swollen veins that met in the wrist,
Under whose brown the amethyst
I longed to taste. I longed to turn
My heart's red measure in her cup,
I longed to feel my hot blood burn
With the amethyst in her cup.

Then suddenly she looked up,
And I was blind in a tawny-gold day,
Till she took her eyes away.
So she came down from above
And emptied my heart of love.
So I held my heart aloft
To the cuckoo that hung like a dove,
And she settled soft

It seemed that I and the morning world
Were pressed cup-shape to take this reiver
Bird who was weary to have furled
Her wings in us,
As we were weary to receive her.

This bird, this rich,
Sumptuous central grain,
This mutable witch,
This one refrain,
This laugh in the fight,
This clot of night,

This core of delight.

She spoke, and I closed my eyes
To shut hallucinations out.
I echoed with surprise
Hearing my mere lips shout
The answer they did devise.

Again I saw a brown bird hover
Over the flowers at my feet;
I felt a brown bird hover
Over my heart, and sweet
Its shadow lay on my heart.
I thought I saw on the clover
A brown bee pulling apart
The closed flesh of the clover
And burrowing in its heart.

She moved her hand, and again
I felt the brown bird cover
My heart; and then
The bird came down on my heart,
As on a nest the rover
Cuckoo comes, and shoves over
The brim each careful part
Of love, takes possession, and settles her down,
With her wings and her feathers to drown
The nest in a heat of love.

She turned her flushed face to me for the glint
Of a moment. "See," she laughed, "if you also
Can make them yawn." I put my hand to the dint
In the flower's throat, and the flower gaped wide
with woe.
She watched, she went of a sudden intensely still,
She watched my hand, to see what I would fulfil.

I pressed the wretched, throttled flower between
My fingers, till its head lay back, its fangs
Poised at her. Like a weapon my hand was white
and keen,
And I held the choked flower-serpent in its pangs
Of mordant anguish, till she ceased to laugh,
Until her pride's flag, smitten, cleaved down to the
staff.

She hid her face, she murmured between her lips
The low word "Don't." I let the flower fall,
But held my hand afloat towards the slips
Of blossom she fingered, and my fingers all
Put forth to her: she did not move, nor I,

For my hand like a snake watched hers, that could
not fly.

Then I laughed in the dark of my heart, I did exult
Like a sudden chuckling of music. I bade her eyes
Meet mine, I opened her helpless eyes to consult
Their fear, their shame, their joy that underlies
Defeat in such a battle. In the dark of her eyes
My heart was fierce to make her laughter rise.

Till her dark deeps shook with convulsive thrills, and
the dark
Of her spirit wavered like water thrilled with light;
And my heart leaped up in longing to plunge its stark
Fervour within the pool of her twilight,
Within her spacious soul, to grope in delight.

And I do not care, though the large hands of revenge
Shall get my throat at last, shall get it soon,
If the joy that they are searching to avenge
Have risen red on my night as a harvest moon,
Which even death can only put out for me;
And death, I know, is better than not-to-be.

A PASSING BELL

Mournfully to and fro, to and fro the trees are
waving;
What did you say, my dear?
The rain-bruised leaves are suddenly shaken, as a
child
Asleep still shakes in the clutch of a sob
Yes, my love, I hear.

One lonely bell, one only, the storm-tossed afternoon
is braving,
Why not let it ring?
The roses lean down when they hear it, the tender,
mild
Flowers of the bleeding-heart fall to the throb
It is such a little thing!

A wet bird walks on the lawn, call to the boy to come
and look,
Yes, it is over now.
Call to him out of the silence, call him to see
The starling shaking its head as it walks in the
Grass
Ah, who knows how?

He cannot see it, I can never show it him, how it
Shook
Don't disturb him, darling.
Its head as it walked: I can never call him to me,
Never, he is not, whatever shall come to pass.
No, look at the wet starling.

IN TROUBLE AND SHAME

I look at the swaling sunset
And wish I could go also
Through the red doors beyond the black-purple bar.

I wish that I could go
Through the red doors where I could put off
My shame like shoes in the porch,
My pain like garments,
And leave my flesh discarded lying
Like luggage of some departed traveller
Gone one knows not where.

Then I would turn round,
And seeing my cast-off body lying like lumber,
I would laugh with joy.

ELEGY

Since I lost you, my darling, the sky has come near,
And I am of it, the small sharp stars are quite near,
The white moon going among them like a white bird
among snow-berries,
And the sound of her gently rustling in heaven like
a bird I hear.

And I am willing to come to you now, my dear,
As a pigeon lets itself off from a cathedral dome
To be lost in the haze of the sky, I would like to
come,
And be lost out of sight with you, and be gone like
foam.

For I am tired, my dear, and if I could lift my feet,
My tenacious feet from off the dome of the earth
To fall like a breath within the breathing wind
Where you are lost, what rest, my love, what rest!

GREY EVENING

When you went, how was it you carried with you
My missal book of fine, flamboyant hours?
My book of turrets and of red-thorn bowers,
And skies of gold, and ladies in bright tissue?

Now underneath a blue-grey twilight, heaped
Beyond the withering snow of the shorn fields
Stands rubble of stunted houses; all is reaped
And garnered that the golden daylight yields.

Dim lamps like yellow poppies glimmer among
The shadowy stubble of the under-dusk,
As farther off the scythe of night is swung,
And little stars come rolling from their husk.

And all the earth is gone into a dust
Of greyness mingled with a fume of gold,
Covered with aged lichens, pale with must,
And all the sky has withered and gone cold.

And so I sit and scan the book of grey,
Feeling the shadows like a blind man reading,
All fearful lest I find the last words bleeding
With wounds of sunset and the dying day.

FIRELIGHT AND NIGHTFALL

The darkness steals the forms of all the queens,
But oh, the palms of his two black hands are red,
Inflamed with binding up the sheaves of dead
Hours that were once all glory and all queens.

And I remember all the sunny hours
Of queens in hyacinth and skies of gold,
And morning singing where the woods are scrolled
And diapered above the chaunting flowers.

Here lamps are white like snowdrops in the grass;
The town is like a churchyard, all so still
And grey now night is here; nor will
Another torn red sunset come to pass.

THE MYSTIC BLUE

Out of the darkness, fretted sometimes in its sleeping,
Jets of sparks in fountains of blue come leaping
To sight, revealing a secret, numberless secrets keeping.

Sometimes the darkness trapped within a wheel
Runs into speed like a dream, the blue of the steel
Showing the rocking darkness now a-reel.

And out of the invisible, streams of bright blue drops
Rain from the showery heavens, and bright blue crops
Surge from the under-dark to their ladder-tops.

And all the manifold blue and joyous eyes,
The rainbow arching over in the skies,
New sparks of wonder opening in surprise.

All these pure things come foam and spray of the sea
Of Darkness abundant, which shaken mysteriously,
Breaks into dazzle of living, as dolphins that leap from the sea
Of midnight shake it to fire, so the secret of death we see.

D H Lawrence – A Short Biography

David Herbert Lawrence was born on the 11th September 1885 to Arthur John Lawrence and Lydia
(née Bearsall). His father was nearly illiterate and his mother trained as a teacher until she was
forced to take a job in a lace factory due to her family's difficult financial situation. He was born in
Eastwood, Nottinghamshire, a coal mining town. There was tension between his parents, likely
stemming from the harsh realities of their life as part of the working class. Lawrence would draw
inspiration from both these aspects of his difficult childhood throughout his artistic career. Indeed,
he wrote about the area, describing it as "the country of [his] heart", and set a large amount of his
fiction there.

As a young boy he was schooled at Beauvale Board School from 1891-98. He was the area's first boy
to win a scholarship from the County Council to attend Nottingham High School, which he did from
1898-1901 at which time he left in favour of a job as a junior clerk in Haywood's surgical appliances
factory. He showed early signs of promise in this career, though it was cut short by a severe case of
pneumonia. He frequently visited Hagg's Farm during his recovery, where he became friends with
Jessie Chambers who lived at the farm with her parents. They shared a love of books, and were part
of a small circle of friends all of whom were avid readers. Lawrence was able to continue his literary
education by engaging in discussion with this group of likeminded adolescents, until he took up a
teacher training position at the British School, Eastwood, from 1902-06. He became a full time
student again and received his teaching qualification in 1908 from University College, Nottingham.
By now he had begun writing and was working on early drafts of his first poems, short stories and a
draft of *Laetitia*, which materialised as *The White Peacock*. His first literary recognition came in the
form of success at a 1907 short story competition held by the *Nottingham Guardian*.

On receiving his qualification from Nottingham University he left for London where he took up a
teaching post in Davidson Road School in Croydon. He continued his writing alongside his teaching

career and soon garnered the attention of Ford Madox Ford, then editor of *The English Review*, an influential literary review. Jessie Chambers had sent the poems in to him and he commissioned Lawrence to write *Odour of Chrysanthemums* which was published in that magazine in 1911. It was noticed by the publishing group Heinemann, who asked Lawrence for more of his writing. Though he continued teaching for a further year, his workload as a published author was sufficient to call this the real beginning of his literary career.

However, his mother had died of cancer shortly before *the White Peacock* was published and this had a profound effect on him, leaving him devastated and incapable of writing for several months, a period of time which he would later describe as his "sick year". The effect of her death on him can be found represented in 1913's *Sons and Lovers*, a work considered largely autobiographical, at the effect of the death of the character Mrs. Morel on her son Paul.

As Lawrence's mourning period ended he was given the private diaries of Helen Corke, his teaching colleague, which contained an account of an unhappy, doomed love affair, which formed the basis of his second novel, *The Trespasser*, which was published in 1912. Meanwhile he was introduced to Edward Garnett, who worked as a publisher's reader, and who became Lawrence's mentor and later friend. He completed the first draft of *Paul Morel*, which became *Sons and Lovers*, under the guidance of Garnett. Lawrence met Frieda Weekley, née von Richthofen, in 1912. She was six years his senior and married to his former modern languages professor at Nottingham, Ernest Weekley, with three young children. Together they eloped to Metz, a garrison town in Germany and home to her parents. It was near to the disputed border with France and there Lawrence witnessed first hand the political and military tension between France and Germany. He was arrested on the accusation of being a spy for the British, though Frieda's father's intervention secured him his release.

Following this incident Lawrence and Frieda relocated to a village near Munich, where they enjoyed a "honeymoon" which later inspired the collection of poems *Look! We Have Come Through!*" which were published in 1917. While here Lawrence completed his first ever play, *The Daughter-in-Law*, which was the first of what he named his 'mining plays'. It was written in Nottingham dialect, and neither performed nor published in his lifetime. They left Germany in the end of 1912 and travelled to Italy across the Alps, a journey later recorded in *Twilight in Italy*, in which "the happiest part of his genius found expression - his curiosity, his spontaneity and the sense of fun he showed more often in life than in his novels". It was while he was in Italy that he finally completed *Sons and Lovers*, though by now he was so exasperated by the novel that he handed it over to Garett without complaint at the knowledge of Garett's intention to cut approximately one hundred pages.

In 1913 Lawrence and Frieda made a brief return visit to Britain where they befriended the critic John Middleton Murry and the popular short story writer Katherine Mansfield. Lawrence also successfully arranged a meeting with W. H. Davies, a Welsh tramp poet, of whose nature-inspired works he was a great admirer. The admiration was in some ways mutual, for Davies, a keen collector of autographs, insisted that he take Lawrence's, perhaps seeing in the young Lawrence the future literary giant he would become. Though Lawrence was so taken by Davies on their meeting that he invited him to visit Frieda and himself in Germany, his opinion changed when he read Davies's *Foliage* and *Nature Poems* and found them to be "so thin, one can hardly feel them". Shortly after this meeting they returned to Italy where they took residence in a cottage in Fiascherino on the Gulf of Spezia. It was while they were staying there that Lawrence began working on the first draft of a novel which would later transform into two of his best-known works, *The Rainbow* (1915) and *Women in Love* (1920).

In early 1914 Frieda obtained her divorce from Ernest Weekley and she and Lawrence returned to Britain to be married on the 13th of July 1914, days before the outbreak of the First World War. At the time of their marriage he was working alongside various intellectual thinkers and writers based in London such as T. S. Eliot, Dora Marsden, Ezra Pound, and others, on *The Egoist*, a pivotal modernist literary magazine in which some of his work was published. He was simultaneously working on an adaptation of Fillipo Tommaso Marinetti's *Futurist Manifesto*, a work which celebrated the machinery and industry of the future, and the violence and speed of youth. Owing to Frieda's German parentage, and his public dislike of militarism and violence, the couple were treated with contempt and suspicion in view of the onset of war with Germany. They were living in Cornwall at this time, in quite severe circumstances, and were accused of spying and signalling to German submarines.

The Rainbow was investigated in 1915 for its profanity and ultimately its publication was suppressed. Lawrence completed *Women in Love* in 1916, though it was not published until 1920 thanks to its bleak view of humanity's destructive tendencies. It is now widely considered to be one of the English language's most finely observed, delicately crafted and subtly intellectual novels.

While he was writing in Cornwall Lawrence began a strong relationship with William Henry Hocking, a farmer. Though the nature of their relationship is unknown, Frieda was convinced that it was sexual. Indeed, homosexuality is an overt theme in *Women in Love*, and Lawrence had previously written in a letter "I should like to know why nearly every man that approaches greatness tends to homosexuality, whether he admits it or not", and "I believe the nearest I've come to perfect love was with a young coal-miner when I was about sixteen." Lawrence and Frieda were constantly hassled by the armed forces authorities throughout the war and in late 1917 they were given three days' notice to leave Cornwall under the terms of the Defence of the Realm Act. He detailed this exile in a chapter of *Kangaroo*, a Australian novel, published in 1923.

The couple moved to Hermitage, a village near the town of Newbury in Berkshire, and then to Derbyshire where they lived out the remainder of the war at Mountain Cottage, Middleton-by-Wirksworth. It was here that he wrote *The White Peacock*. The couple were extremely poor and Lawrence almost succumbed to a bout of influenza as they could barely afford adequate medical attention.

Lawrence's reputation in England was by now heavily tarnished, met only by his own disdain for the country. He and Frieda flew the country in November 1919, the earliest politically possible opportunity, and made for Abruzzi in Italy before continuing to Capri and the Fontana Vecchia in Taormina, Sicily. From there he travelled widely across Europe including Sardinia, Malta, Austria and Germany. Much of this period of travelling is detailed in his writing, particularly in *Twilight in Italy*. He called his travelling his 'savage pilgrimage' and considered it a voluntary exile from Britain. He only returned to Britain twice in the rest of his life, each time for a brief visit. Instead, he and Frieda spent the remainder of their lives travelling, reaching Australia, Ceylon, Mexico and the United States. He continued his fiction alongside his travel writing, winning the James Tait Black Memorial Prize for fiction for 1920's *The Lost Girl*. He wrote short stories such as *The Captain's Doll*, *The Ladybird* and *The Fox*, poetry such as that collected in *Birds, Beasts and Flowers*, and several travel journals, particularly *Sea and Sardinia*. He was obliged to publish his textbook *Movements in European History* under a pseudonym owing to his unfavourable reputation in England.

Lawrence and Frieda departed for America in February 1922, sailing East to Ceylon (Sri Lanka) and on to Australia. While in Australia Lawrence completed *Kangaroo*, dealing with local politics and his experience of the war in England. They continued to America and arrived in September of that year, acquiring Kiowa Ranch in New Mexico, making payment with the manuscript of *Sons and Lovers*.

They made their final visit to England at the end of 1923 but quickly returned to their ranch, considering his life and career in England effectively over. In March 1925 he visited Mexico and suffered a severe attack of malaria which nearly killed him. He was instructed to convalesce in Europe and so he and Frieda returned to Italy where they took a home in a villa near Florence. Here he wrote *The Virgin and the Gypsy* and *Lady Chatterley's Lover*, which brought renewed notoriety to his name for its controversially sexual subject matter. He addressed his critics head on with satirical poems and a piece entitled *Pornography and Obscenity*. While in Italy he bolstered his friendship with the author Aldous Huxley and renewed his interest in oil painting. An exhibition in 1929 was raided by the police and several works confiscated.

David Herbert Lawrence died of complications arising from a bout of tuberculosis on the 2nd of March 1930 in Vence, France.

D. H. Lawrence – A Concise Bibliography

Novels
The White Peacock (1911)
The Trespasser (1912)
Sons and Lovers (1913)
The Rainbow (1915)
Women in Love (1920)
The Lost Girl (1920)
Aaron's Rod (1922)
Kangaroo (1923)
The Boy in the Bush (1924)
The Plumed Serpent (1926)
Lady Chatterley's Lover (1928)
The Escaped Cock (1929), later re-published as The Man Who Died

Short Story Collections
The Prussian Officer and Other Stories (1914)
England, My England and Other Stories (1922)
The Horse Dealer's Daughter (1922)
The Fox, The Captain's Doll, The Ladybird (1923)
St Mawr and other stories (1925)
The Woman who Rode Away and other stories (1928)
The Rocking-Horse Winner (1926)
The Virgin and the Gipsy and Other Stories (1930)
Love Among the Haystacks and other stories (1930)

Poetry Collections
Love Poems and others (1913)
Amores (1916)
Look! We have come through! (1917)
New Poems (1918)
Bay: a book of poems (1919)
Tortoises (1921)

Birds, Beasts and Flowers (1923)
The Collected Poems of D H Lawrence (1928)
Pansies (1929)
Nettles (1930)
Last Poems (1932)
Fire and other poems (1940)

Plays

The Daughter-in-Law (1912)
The Widowing of Mrs Holroyd (1914)
Touch and Go (1920)
David (1926)
The Fight for Barbara (1933)
A Collier's Friday Night (1934)
The Married Man (1940)
The Merry-Go-Round (1941)

Non Fiction & Pamphlets

Study of Thomas Hardy and other essays (1914),
Movements in European History (1921),
Psychoanalysis and the Unconscious and Fantasia of the Unconscious (1921/1922)
Studies in Classic American Literature (1923)
Reflections on the Death of a Porcupine and other essays (1925)
A Propos of Lady Chatterley's Lover (1929)
Apocalypse and the writings on Revelation (1931)
Phoenix: The Posthumous Papers of D. H. Lawrence (1936)

Travel Books

Twilight in Italy and Other Essays (1916)
Sea and Sardinia (1921)
Mornings in Mexico and Other Essays (1927),
Sketches of Etruscan Places and other Italian essays (1932)

Works translated by Lawrence

Lev Isaakovich Shestov All Things are Possible (1920)
Ivan Alekseyevich Bunin The Gentleman from San Francisco (1922), tr. with S. S. Koteliansky
Giovanni Verga Mastro-Don Gesualdo (1923)
Giovanni Verga Little Novels of Sicily (1925)
Giovanni Verga Cavalleria Rusticana and other stories (1928)
Antonio Francesco Grazzini The Story of Doctor Manente (1929)

Manuscripts and early drafts of published novels and other works

Paul Morel (1911–12), an early manuscript version of Sons and Lovers
The First Women in Love (1916–17)
Mr Noon, (unfinished novel) Parts I and II
The Symbolic Meaning: The Uncollected Versions of Studies in Classic American Literature
Quetzalcoatl (1925), edited by Louis L Martz. Early draft of The Plumed Serpent

The First and Second Lady Chatterley novels

Paintings
The Paintings of D. H. Lawrence, London: Mandrake Press, 1929.

www.ingramcontent.com/pod-product-compliance
Lightning Source LLC
Chambersburg PA
CBHW070810120626
46557CB00002B/804